POWER RANGERS
MYSTIC FORCE

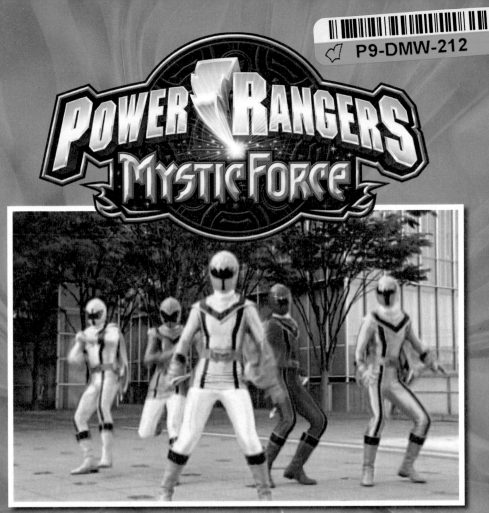

RANGERS IN DANGER

Adapted by Tisha Hamilton

ISBN-13: 978-0-439-92540-2   ISBN-10: 0-439-92540-1
Power Rangers: ™ & © BVS Entertainment, Inc. and BVS International N.V. All Rights Reserved.
Published by Scholastic Inc.
SCHOLASTIC and associated logos are trademarks and/or registered trademarks of Scholastic Inc.
12 11 10 9 8 7 6 5 4 3 2   7 8 9 10 11/0
Printed in the U.S.A.   First printing, November 2007

SCHOLASTIC INC.

New York   Toronto   London   Auckland   Sydney
Mexico City   New Delhi   Hong Kong   Buenos Aires

The evil Imperious had a plan to destroy the city—and the Power Rangers. He gave Jester a magic pen. "I know just what to do," Jester promised.

Clare, a friend of the Rangers, saw the danger in the crystal ball at Rootcore, the Ranger headquarters.

"There's a creature attacking people in Briarwood!" she called out.

The Rangers took off to tackle Jester. No one noticed the green frog on Madison's shoulder.

Clare gasped when she looked back at the crystal ball. "Now it's showing Dark Magic right here!" she said.

Udonna, the Rangers' teacher, came over to look. But before she could see it, Udonna's friend Calindor touched the crystal ball. It went clear.

Clare was worried. Could Calindor be causing the dark magic?

In Briarwood, the Rangers battled Jester. But then he vanished!

All they found was a strange mark Jester had painted on the sidewalk. What could it mean?

Back at Ranger headquarters, Udonna told her friend Calindor about the Xenotome. "The Rangers' powers come from the Xenotome. It is all-knowing." Calindor handed Udonna a mug of tea.

Clare did not trust Calindor. She knocked the mug away. The tea was poisoned!

"I guess this game is over," Calindor said. Then he morphed into his true form: Imperious!

Imperious froze Clare and Udonna with a spell. Then he tried to take the Xenotome! But Udonna had enchanted it. Calindor could not steal it—yet.

In Briarwood, Jester had returned.
"Who wants to see a trick?" he called. People screamed and ran to get away from him.

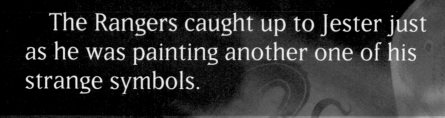

The Rangers caught up to Jester just as he was painting another one of his strange symbols.

Madison didn't waste any time. "Water power!" she shouted. Her powerful blast washed away Jester's mark.

Madison had figured out Jester's plan. Jester's symbols would make a dark seal around the city. But the Rangers would not let that happen. "You're going down!" Madison shouted to Jester.

Jester's next blast demorphed Madison. Without her Power Ranger protection, she was defenseless, and Jester was ready to blast her again.

Then the tiny frog on Madison's shoulder took a mighty hop. It distracted Jester, and he missed!

Madison hated frogs, but this one was special. "You saved my life," she whispered. Then she kissed the frog and something strange began to happen.

The frog morphed into a handsome warrior.
It was Daggeron!

"Thanks," he said to Madison. "You broke the curse."

"Stand back," Daggeron said. He pulled out a solar morpher and transformed into Solaris Knight with the power of the sun.

Daggeron turned his blaster on Jester.

Jester tried to hide underground, but Solaris Knight's blaster beam followed him.

Solaris Knight aimed the Lamp Blaster again. This time, it was a direct hit!

As Solaris Knight demorphed into Daggeron, the Rangers crowded around. "You rock!" they exclaimed.

"Who are you?" Madison wanted to know.

"No time for that now," Daggeron said. "Udonna's in trouble!"

Daggeron and the Rangers took off for Rootcore.

Imperious had finally broken Udonna's spell. He was reaching for the Xenotome when a powerful blast knocked him sideways. The blast also freed Clare and Udonna.

Udonna couldn't believe Daggeron was back. He explained how Calindor had betrayed him during the Great Battle. Ever since, Daggeron had been trapped in the body of a frog—until Madison broke the spell.

Imperious did not stay and fight. "We will meet again," he threatened. "And next time you will fall!" Then he vanished in a puff of smoke.

The Power Rangers had defeated evil
once again! And now they had a new ally:
Daggeron.